DISNEY'S
THE NEW ADVENTURES OF
WINNIE the POOH
The Masked Offender

Twin Books

MALLARD PRESS

It was a beautiful, sunny day in the Hundred-Acre Wood. Tigger was sitting under a tree, reading his favorite comic book.

"Through the countryside raced the Lord High Mayor's carriage," read Tigger.

"Faster and faster the coachman drove, cracking his whip, nervously looking over his shoulder, knowing that somewhere out there waited the most dreaded bandit of them all... "EL CONEJO!"

"Suddenly, there he was! El Conejo! 'Halt!' yelled the bandit. The driver drew back on the reins and pulled the brake handle. Passengers strained at their safety belts, brakes squealed, dust flew, and the carriage ground to a halt!"

Tigger turned the page.

"'Your honey or your life!' snarled El Conejo.

"'Not my *honey*!' stammered the Lord High Mayor."

"'Have no fear, citizens!' yelled a voice from a nearby tree. 'It is I, the Masked Avenger!'

"The masked hero swung down heroically and landed in the road in front of El Conejo. The bandit fled in panic at the mere sight of the Masked Avenger."

"Boy, I'd love to be just like that Masked Offender," exclaimed Tigger, bouncing with enthusiasm. "What a guy! What a hero! Just like a tigger, on account of he's the only one!"

Later that day, Piglet heard a knock at his door. When he opened it, there stood the Masked Offender (who was really Tigger in disguise).

"Greetings, citizen!" said Tigger. "You have the honor of being my faithful sidekick!"

"B-b-but...who are you?" asked Piglet.

"I am the Masked Offender," declared Tigger, "and I need you to do all the important sidekicky stuff, like carryin' my hero suit!"

"Oh, really?" asked Piglet, enthusiastically.

Nearby, Rabbit was working in his garden. From a nearby bush, the Masked Offender and his faithful sidekick watched.

"Look, faithful sidekick!" urged the Masked Offender. "An evildoer is sneakin' up on bunny boy!"

"That's no evildoer," said Piglet, "it's only a scarecrow."

But before Piglet could finish his sentence, the Masked Offender had bounded from the bushes.

"Masked Offender to the rescue!" cried Tigger.

Without warning, the Masked Offender pounced on the scarecrow, tearing it to shreds. Rabbit ducked as bits of scarecrow flew all over the place.

When he was done, Tigger posed heroically over the
shredded scarecrow.

Rabbit stammered, "Wh-what…b-b-but…my scarecrow!"

"No need for thanks, citizen," said the Masked Offender.

"But now the crows will eat everything in my garden!"
blubbered Rabbit.

"Masked Offender awaaayyyy!" cried Tigger, and with a
swirl of his cape, he bounded off into the woods.

Soon the Masked Offender and his faithful sidekick were standing in front of Gopher's home.

"Look! Gopher's roof is full of holes," observed Tigger. "When it rains, he'll be flooded! We gotta save him, quick!"

Then the Masked Offender filled up Gopher's holes and bounced up and down to pack the dirt in.

Gopher stuck his head out from another hole. He was all covered with dirt.

"Sssay, what's goin' on here, sssonny?" asked Gopher.

"No need for thanks, citizen," said Tigger. "Masked Offender awaaayyyy!" And he was gone!

Later his faithful sidekick found the Masked Offender sawing away at a big tree.

"But there's no one here to rescue," Piglet pointed out.

"Sure there is, faithful sidekick," said the Masked Offender. "Obviously this tree grew up under Owl's house when he wasn't lookin'. He's in terrible danger. If he sleepwalks, he might fall and break his beak."

Just then, Owl's house tilted and fell, *CRASH!*

The next day, Rabbit, Gopher, Owl, and Pooh all met to decide what to do about the Masked Offender.

"He fed my garden to the crows!" said Rabbit.

"He destroyed my home!" growled Gopher.

"Mine, too!" screeched Owl.

"Let's give him a taste of his own medicine!" said Rabbit.

"I sssecond the motion!" said Gopher.

"I third and fourth it!" said Owl.

From a nearby bush, Piglet witnessed the whole thing.

"Oh, d-d-dear! I must warn the Masked Offender!" exclaimed Piglet.

Piglet found Tigger on top of a hill. "Masked Offender," he said, "our friends don't like what you're doing."

Suddenly someone cried, "Help us, Masked Offender!"

"Oh, yeah?" said Tigger. "Listen—somebody needs me. Masked Offender to the rescue!"

The Masked Offender found Rabbit, Owl, Gopher and Pooh running around and screaming.

"Help! It's horrible!" screamed Rabbit.

"It's a whatchamadingle!" screeched Owl.

"And it's in the bushes!" added Pooh.

Tigger dashed into the bushes.

Tigger came face to face with the whatchamadingle.
"Yuck! There's a face only a mother whatchamadingle could love! So, you're the bully who's been bullyin' my friends, eh? All right, put up your dukes! Masked Offender awaaayyyy!"

With a flurry of furry fury, the Masked Offender flew into the whatchamadingle like a tigger. Clouds of dust, fur, branches, and bits of whatchamadingle flew everywhere.

And when the dust cleared, the Masked Offender was stuck to the whatchamadingle like a fly to flypaper. Tigger and the whatchamadingle were one big, gooey mass of drippy glue.

Rabbit, Owl, and Gopher all laughed hysterically.

"Oh, Masked Offender, you saved us!" laughed Rabbit sarcastically.

"Are you all right?" asked Piglet.

"I'm fine, Piglet," said Tigger as he untied his Masked Offender costume and stepped out of it. He jumped down to the ground and landed with a bounce.

"Tigger!" gasped Rabbit in disbelief. "Tigger is the Masked Offender?"

"I didn't know Tigger was the masked offender!" said Owl.

"Neither did I!" cried Gopher.

"I guess you were right, Piglet," sighed Tigger. "Nobody wants a Masked Offender."

With his shoulders drooping, the downcast Tigger headed for home.

Suddenly the whatchamadingle started rolling.

It rolled right over Rabbit, Owl, Gopher, and Pooh. It rolled down the hill and headed for the Hundred-Acre Canyon.

Faster and faster the whatchamadingle rolled, with the whole gang attached, screaming and yelling.

And they rolled right past Piglet, just missing him.

The bouncing ball of gluey goo rumbled out onto the bridge over Hundred-Acre Canyon and got snagged on one of the splintery slats of the rickety old bridge.

Dangling like a yo-yo over Hundred-Acre Canyon, Rabbit, Owl, Gopher, and Pooh started hollering for help.

Piglet dashed to Tigger's house.
"Tigger! Tigger!" screamed Piglet. "The others are in danger! It looks like a job for the Masked Offender!"

"Sorry, pal," said Tigger, moping in the corner. "Nothin' doin'. They don't need me. Besides, I don't have my hero suit anymore!"

"Well, if you're not going to help our friends," said Piglet, "I will!" Grabbing a dishtowel, Piglet dashed out the front door. "Piglet awaaayyyy!" he yelled, and zipped off.

Worried about his former sidekick, Tigger stepped to the door in time to see his little pal disappear over the hill.

"'Piglet away'?" he muttered.

Before he knew it, Piglet was stuck in the gluey goo with all his friends. All he could do was join them in yelling for help.

Suddenly, from a nearby tree, came a very welcome greeting.

"Have no fear, citizens! Tigger awaaayyyy!"

Tigger tied a rope to a nearby tree. He swung out from the tree and hit the ball of gluey goo full-force. He stuck firmly to it, as only a tigger could. Then he pulled and pulled on his rope with all his might, and the gluey goo stretched like a rubber band.

It finally snapped and shot them all the way back to Pooh's house. They hit Pooh's house with such force that they all popped free of the ball of gluey goo.

Tigger felt sorry for all the trouble he had caused, and spent the next day repairing everybody's house.

"If the Masked Offender were here," said Tigger, "he'd have this done in no time."

"Now, Tigger," warned Piglet, "remember what happened last time."

Tigger went back to work, realizing that he was a better tigger than he was a masked offender.